THE **POISON** OF **WAR**

by Jennifer Leeper

prensa press

Library of Congress Control Number: 2019947391

ISBN: 978-1-7332402-0-8 (Paperback Edition)
ISBN: 978-1-7332402-1-5 (e-book)

Published by Prensa Press
Mexico City, Mexico · Chicago, IL
www.prensa.press
info@prensa.press

Distributed by Ingram Publisher Services

Cover design and illustrations copyright © by Polly Jiménez
Book design by Polly Jiménez
Editing by Paul Biasco

First paperback edition November 2019
Printed in the United States of America

Visit www.thepoisonofwar.com

THE **POISON** OF **WAR**

by Jennifer Leeper

Tohono O'odham Nation Territory

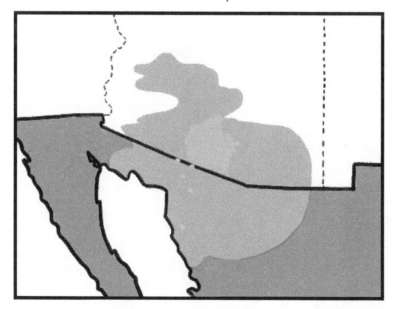

CHAPTER
1

The two bodies lay in plain sight of the shuttered Salt Bingo Casino, though there were no witnesses other than a coyote and its jackrabbit prey. The two bodies lay still until the sun cracked its light over the Arizona desert like a great sky egg.

A pair of hikers discovered Joaquin Carrillo and Diego Velazquez weighted with eight pounds of Mexican-grown heroin on a Sunday morning. They lay in the upper Sonora on the periphery of the Tohono O'odham Indian Reservation. A single arrow pierced a vital organ inside each of the deceased.

Detective Frank Silva examined the entry site of an arrow lodged in Joaquin's left gut, eyeing a matching arrow in Diego's side. Frank rose slowly on aging knees. A gray and black braid snaked down the back of his denim shirt.

"Not even a footprint," Frank muttered to himself. "And they left the wallets and heroin, so it wasn't a payday. Could be a message to someone."

"The high school kids are making bows the old way now." Detective Arturo Vega nodded toward the bodies. He stood several inches shorter than his older partner, his black hair shaved close to his head. The men shared the wide, sweeping features of Papago-Pima ancestry.

"I thought they shot with compounds," said Frank moving out of the way of the body as a crime scene technician began dusting for prints. His feet kicked up dust as he looked for indications of a struggle such as smashed vegetation or blood. There wasn't so much as a bent prickly pear pad, though, and the only red came from the natural stain of desert ground around the crime scene.

"For their college archery scholarship money, but they shoot the old way when they're chasing down rabbits," said Arturo, trickling his dark eyes up the length of the bodies. "I've seen 'em with these." The younger detective ran a gloved finger through the colorful fletching of one of the arrows. "Used with old recurve bows."

"These kids want their full rides to AU. They wouldn't risk using that kind of weapon." Frank spoke in the flat, broad vowels of the Tohono O'odham people.

Arturo's sad, drooping eyes softened the otherwise hard lines of his face. "They're young and immortal. Nothing to risk and everything to gain from sending a message to the cartel."

"We'll see if prints turn up, but I'll talk with Graham and Russell to start. They're the best, right?" Frank said, keeping his hunch about suspects other than high school kids warm in his thoughts.

·》》·✦·《《·

Frank raised a fist to knock, but the forensics lab door opened before he made contact.

"Poison," the tech reported.

"The arrowheads." Frank stated as much as asked.

"Paralyzed both victims." The tech handed Frank a multiple-page report confirming what the detective already suspected.

Frank flipped through the report, quickly scanning each page. "It's an old recipe."

The tech nodded. "Used for tribal warfare. Our people used it. So did the Mohaves, Apaches, and a few other tribes. No prints."

"I might've guessed. Thanks."

Frank wandered back to his office where two of the best archers on the reservation would be waiting for him.

·»»·✦·««·

The two boys sat still in the waiting room of
the Tohono O'odham Nation police headquarters.
Though they shared some of the same bold features,
the boys were opposites. Frank studied them through
the blinds of his office window before calling them in.

A one-dimensional mohawk striped sixteen-
year-old Graham Soto's skull. He rubbed his palms
several times on the tops of his faded jeans as if they
were sweaty. Graham's broad physique overwhelmed a
too-fitted white t-shirt.

A thick dark braid reached the middle of
fifteen-year-old Russell Torres's spine. He wore a black
t-shirt—featuring the name of a Tohono O'odham
rock band—and jeans. On his feet were traditional
Papago-style moccasins with missing beadwork here
and there.

"Russell." Frank swept the boy into his office
with serious eyes.

Russell entered and sat, bouncing the tips of
his fingers on his thighs. The boy's thin fingers popping
up and down reminded Frank of the boy's thin-light
presence in general. He could imagine Russell barely
tethered to gravity, moving along desert ground,
perfectly formed for stalking other living creatures with
a bow and arrow.

"How come I'm not in that room down the
hall?" Russell asked.

Frank shook his head. "I knew your grandfather and your father. I don't need a special room for my questions." Frank could see the boy understood—he was more like an uncle interrogating him.

The detective leaned back in his chair. "You heard about what happened?"

Russell nodded. "It's why we're here, right?" His pogo-stick fingers finally rested as he stilled. "You think we did it."

Frank had chosen to break open dialogue with the boys through Russell because of candor like this. Graham appeared to have more of a presence than the smaller boy, but that was a default presumption.

Frank smiled. "I don't think you or Graham killed anyone. But maybe you know someone who's just as quick and just as accurate as you. Maybe someone who taught you how to make bows in the old way."

Frank nodded coaxingly while Russell focused on chewing the nail of an index finger. Frank couldn't tell if it was a nervous twitch or just a habit.

"What about your coach?" Frank tried not to notice the indicators of youth in the boy as this could distract him to an overly biased sympathy toward a child who also happened to be a suspect. Instead he considered his own aging body with its extra rings of fat around his middle, arthritic joints and even the scars of injuries mapping time across his body.

Russell met Frank's gaze again. There was no surprise in the boy's eyes at Frank's unsubtle trap. "You know he was the first to get a full ride for archery in our district. And you know he's just as good, so why ask?" Russell straightened his posture, matching the confidence of his gaze.

"He never took his ride. He decided to stay in Rainmaker District and train up another generation. Your coach train you on live targets or bags and trees?"

Russell sighed through his nose. "Bags and trees and sometimes coyote and Javelina."

Frank leaned forward over his desk, a loud creak from his chair announcing his growing midsection and interest in the boy's responses. "So at night—in the desert, with longbows?"

Russell nodded, compressing his lips.

"I've talked to some of the other coaches around the county, and none of them train that way."

It's legal."

"I didn't say it was illegal."

"He didn't do it."

"That's what I'm trying to discover for myself." The older boy would tell him the same, in more or less words. "What about poison arrowheads? He ever teach you any recipes?"

A tensed jaw muscle locked in defiance across Russell's broad features. "No." The single word echoed against the boy's hardened expression of wide, immovable cheekbones and too-still eyes and lips.

Frank knew the boy was telling the truth as far as he understood it, but he also knew Coach Emilio.

Emilio's grandfather was a shaman who knew how to make the arrowhead—the one used in war with the Apache that poisoned the River People. He also knew of Emilio's public anger at the drug traffickers.

"Go ahead and send Graham in."

Russell got up to leave but turned around. "Graham doesn't know anything either." The defiance lifted only long enough to slip his words past a still-clenched jaw.

He shut the door behind him before Frank could respond.

Frank leaned back in his chair, closing his eyes, then opening them to the darkness of reflection. Arturo would want to question the boys too. He would seed his questioning with a bias toward the outcome he wanted just as Frank had done, and he would still come up empty. If only the desert could talk. Frank would settle for questioning Emilio.

⋅»⟩ ⋅✦⋅ ⟨«⋅

Emilio Acuna sat in the last pew of St. Ignatius, his head down.

Behind Emilio, Frank smelled the air of the sanctuary, a lingering aroma of incense seducing his memory with images of his veiled mother entering the Confessional, her lips shaping the prayer born of the

Virgin's fiat. St. Ignatius was less than a century old, built over the site of a Spanish mission that existed in the 1700s through the early nineteenth century. Mexican militia destroyed the old mission church as part of a forced claim on the southernmost territories of Arizona.

So many had tried to claim Papago lands.

St. Ignatius's priest, Father Jim Harris, was half Papago and respected in the community.

"Never thought I'd see you in here." The unhurried vowels of an indigenous speaker fringed with highbrow British turned Frank's and Emilio's heads. A sweet aroma of cigar smoke wafted from the cleric.

Father Harris stood up to his neck in black with a flash of white at his Adam's apple. His cassock gave his presence a somewhat medieval context. Like Frank, he wore his gray and white hair braided down his back.

Emilio crossed himself and rose, making his way to the other two men. "He's here for me."

The coach, squat-framed and muscular, had a natural amiability in his large dark eyes. Unlike the priest, his features were heavy and wide.

"Emilio needs to see me first." Father Harris's tea-colored eyes jested, his hitchhiker's thumb pointing back at the freestanding wooden box.

Frank grinned out of one side of his mouth. "Maybe I'll put my ear to the wood and get what I need."

"Render unto Caesar, Padre. I don't think I'll

be long with the detective." Emilio lightly clapped the priest on his back.

"Can't promise that."

The side smile disappeared.

Though the priest's eyes were serene, the amusement had expired on his face, a unique contortion in those parts of Anglo and American Indian with his dark skin and fine bone structure. "I'll be waiting."

Emilio followed Frank out of the church.

The two men were soon shrouded in a dry, desert wind, only interrupted in one instance by an all-too-intimate sssss of a snake. Frank noticed the glossy creature coiled under the bright yellow spray of Desert Marigold. Though it wasn't venomous, the reptile was a reminder to be alert for more dangerous species always on the move in the surface stillness of the Sonoran.

"I've known you as long as you've had breath," Frank began once they were a good distance away.

"Then you don't need to question me." Emilio stood in a wide stance, arms folded.

"I know you hate, and you have a bad temper. That's a lethal combination."

"Don't you get pissed off? The cartel uses our land for mule running and kidnaps our people for their drug fields and rapes our women. They make addicts out of the kids around here. They make it hard for us to pass through our own lands. Don't you have family down south? You ever see them? Maybe you put the poisoned arrows in those bastards. No one would question you—you have a badge to hide behind," Emilio accused.

The older man smiled inside at the passion in the younger man. His own passion had flattened with age, and he admired Emilio's, but he knew it was dangerous. "My blood is old. It doesn't boil like yours. Just because I carry a gun doesn't mean I like to use it. Haven't shot an arrow in more than thirty years."

"So you want to know where I was and who I was with and what I was doing and how I was doing it that night? Well, I was sleeping and you know as well as I do I was doing it alone." Bitterness tinged Emilio's words. "Regina left for a white man in Silver." His face guarded his feelings well, but his tone didn't.

"Sorry. I knew you were separated. I hadn't heard the rest." Frank added a small frown to the naturally sympathetic droop at the outer corners of his eyes.

"I haven't told many people but figured you knew."

Though Frank felt sorry for Emilio, his mind scavenged for motive possibly buried in the emotion around a marriage breaking up. He hated suspecting a man he had known from as far back as his time in his mother's belly. "The poison we found on the arrows . . ." Frank paused to gauge Emilio's reaction.

Emilio frowned, but Frank couldn't tell whether it was a reaction to the talk about the younger man's failed marriage.

"He never taught me," Emilio answered Frank's

half question, flattening his frown to a straight, serious lip line.

"Other than a couple of old women," Frank said, "you're the only one raised on the old ways."

"Even if he had taught me, anyone can look up that shit now," Emilio responded.

"But hate belongs to those who own it," Frank retorted.

Emilio straightened his posture, his highly defined body a single taut muscle. "Then we all own it here." Emilio kicked a rock he'd been moving around with his foot.

"Maybe." Frank looked at the pinkish stone suddenly and violently sprung, considering the anger behind the action.

Emilio shook his head. "You want a sacrificial lamb—not a suspect. I'm not a fucking lamb, but I'm not your wolf either."

"Can you take me to the militia?" Frank said, ignoring Emilio's defensive remark.

"We train with guns, not arrows, at the border."

"But a few are your former students?"

"I never taught anyone to hate."

"You don't have to—it's in your eyes."

Frank tried to forget the child he had known, looming behind the man who stood before him. He had survived on blind spots as a reservation detective. This was just one more blind spot he had to sustain through the life of a case.

"Meet me at the community center tomorrow at noon and I'll take you to a training."

"Are you preparing to defend the border or are you preparing for war?" Frank shouted as Emilio walked back toward the church.

Emilio spoke without stopping or turning around. "Both."

Taken at face value, the San Felipe Gate didn't deserve the official status of gate as Frank had always thought. No more than a light pole, one guard, and a few pieces of barbed wire, it was the most naked part of the 1,969-mile U.S.-Mexico border. But now it wore the anger of eleven districts of Tohono O'odham. More than sixty men and women and a few teenagers who had come every other day for nearly a year to train for a battle that had thus far played out bloodlessly in their minds.

An elder just feet from the official border—which other than the single guard inside his booth, looked as lonely as a wire perimeter edging a ranch or farm—spoke to the militia in Spanish.

"Our Desert People passed like wind across this border for hundreds of years until the white man dropped a curtain so we might be divided—divided from family but never from our ancestors. We must become a stronger wind and be guided by the ancestors and most of all by Se'ehe in all of our movements . . ."

Frank understood, and visibly revered the man as he joined the crowd of armed men and women and several teenagers. He recognized many faces, including Graham's and Russell's.

Frank acknowledged other familiar faces with nods as he made his way over to where the boys stood off to the side of the other militia members near an ancient saguaro plant. "I thought you boys only shot arrows."

The boys remained serious despite a half smile pushing up one side of Frank's face.

"Plenty of kids their age here," Emilio said as he approached.

"What's that?" Frank pointed with his eyes at a figure off to the side of the militia gathering. He wandered toward a crude wire rendering of a person.

"The Martyr." Emilio shadowed Frank. "He's not the ghost of the man who killed those two traffickers because we don't know if he's still alive, but he's probably dead because those narco fuckers can find anyone. You wanna question him?" Emilio smiled, but Frank was serious staring into the soulless eyes, wondering if this case would wind up as empty.

"Who made it?" Frank asked.

Emilio pointed in the general direction of the militia. "All guilty."

"All archers too?" Frank spoke to The Martyr because his mind had not fully processed its existence, particularly in the context of the case.

Emilio shook his head. "About half. Half of those are shit and wouldn't know what to do with a longbow. About ten are good and four of those are kids. You've already talked to Graham and Russell."

Frank finally looked back at Emilio. "Give me the other eight then."

"You won't get your lamb here." Emilio's right hand moved to rest on a holstered gun at his side. It rested without the slightest twitch, but Frank took it as the younger man's show of protectiveness of his militia.

Frank looked back into The Martyr's unseeing eyes.

"Let's see."

Emilio rejoined the group and whispered into the ear of a muscular Indian who stood at least a foot above everyone else. When Emilio stopped whispering, the large Indian moved toward Frank.

"I know you." Frank offered his hand, and the younger man accepted it, but his large brown eyes revealed a distrust the detective had seen often on the reservation. It was no more than a reflex, though.

"Your cousin is married to my cousin," the wall said.

Frank remembered. "You're Benito."

Benito nodded, the wariness lifting from his expression. "You wanna know where I was the night of the murder, right? I was sleeping at my girlfriend's house."

"How long has the militia been training?" Frank asked.

"Less than a year—about nine months maybe. They didn't like it at first, but they don't give a shit now." Benito pointed at the lone border guard who casually chatted with one of the militia members, even smiling at intervals. "Anyway, we're basically fighting against the same thing they are."

Frank wondered if the border guards really didn't give a shit about the militia being a presence at the border.

"You're good with a longbow?" Though he listened attentively, Frank studied Benito's body language as much as he absorbed what he said.

Benito raised an eyebrow at the mention of the old-bow style. "I used to win competitions in school, and I got a scholarship, but college wasn't for me. I still shoot but mostly small game on the weekends and bags."

He spoke confidently, without hesitation.

Frank couldn't help but notice the size and evident strength of Benito's arms, which could easily have taken down two men with a more primitive bow. "But you're not just training for bags and rabbits down here."

Time stood still on the Indian's face for a bloated second. "No, not for rabbits . . ." Benito's voice drifted off as Frank's eyes moved to The Martyr. He silently interrogated the wire man, who revealed nothing.

"Okay, Benito," Frank said, "you can send over the next archer."

The other seven fell under the weight of solid alibis. Frank's thoughts returned to its cul-de-sac of Emilio Acuna as he stared into the hollow eyes of The Martyr.

Arturo wiped the shine of the Sonoran heat from his forehead, avoiding Diego Rivera's cartoonish, bulging eyes made more grotesque by the lack of a body. Diego left behind a seventeen-year-old daughter and a wife. A new film of sweat quickly formed at the thought of having to deliver the message of this gruesome death to Diego's wife, now his widow, and daughter.

Frank approached, walling off his nostrils and mouth from the stench of death with a hand. "Caballo Negro Cartel," Frank reported.

"Carrillo and Velazquez must've been more important than we thought," Arturo observed. "Everyone loved Diego."

"Favored cousins of Badillo."

"Where's that coming from?" Arturo asked.

"I'll give you one guess."

"Feds?"

Frank nodded.

"So we're benched?"

Frank shook his head. "Just moved around in the game."

"Meaning?" Arturo folded his arms, widening his stance.

"We'll straddle both cases, but they'll put us in where they want us."

"Of course they will. If you can call this a fucking case." The younger man's nostrils flared in the direction of Diego's remains. "No one will ever be prosecuted."

Frank shrugged, but then shook his head. "Probably not."

Arturo sighed. "I've gotta go knock on a door."

Frank watched Arturo walk away, lighting a cigarette while staring out at the dry sea of desert stretching toward the border. He wondered how much longer a single guard and a light pole could hold back the anger of a people.

·»»·✦·««·

The priest stooped to examine the yellow blossoms on a squash plant. "There she is." Fully cassocked, Father Harris pointed at a small, yellowish squash. "When I came back here from Manchester, this garden helped me feel at home. My father taught me everything about growing veg."

"And shooting?" Frank stood at the edge of the modest rectory garden.

"Yes." The priest straightened. "But so did my mother." Though his words abruptly pinballed between remnants of British and Papago, a calm threaded both accents. Frank had always admired this serenity about priests.

"I remember her. She had a fruit stand off Route 9. My mother always bought blackberries." Frank noticed the graying temples on the priest. "I think you were a grade ahead of me. You left for England in primary, right?"

"Sounds about right. Did you take general science with Mr. Yazzie? He loved to show those old movies about the atomic bombs. You know my father worked on the testing here." Though he looked in Frank's direction, Father Harris's eyes watched something Frank couldn't see—something projected in memory. "They dropped the Fat Man on Nagasaki not a month later." Father Harris stooped to prune a squash plant with overzealous leaf growth.

"My grandfather never hunted there because he said the air had poisoned the animals. It was more superstition than anything. I wasn't raised in the old ways like he raised my father. He didn't teach me those things, but my mother did behind his back."

A playful mischief conjured a smile on Frank's face. "Sounds like we were raised the same way. My mother taught me about talking to the spirits of the dead, and my father told me a very different story about the world."

Frank noticed that for a man his age, the priest straightened his body quickly and couldn't help but apply this agility to the context of his case.

"And we both hear confessions." Frank knew he wasn't being subtle, so at the least he hoped a little humor would buffer his overtness.

"Is that why you're here today, detective?" The priest wiped sweat from his forehead with the back of a garden-gloved hand.

"I was taught to respect the Confessional seal, but if you've heard something outside your box, it's fair game." Frank moved as close to the garden as possible without actually stepping into the beds of vegetables.

"Emilio is passionate, but so are many more, and I count myself among them." The priest bent his body again to remove a dead flower from a squash plant. "There's what I can say outside the box."

"But you haven't joined a militia."

"Not yet." Half-smiling wrinkles softened Father Harris's serious eyes.

Amusement played on Frank's face, but when the priest's expression didn't change, the amusement drooped. "If you do happen to hear something, you know where to find me."

"Maybe one of these days you'll show up at Ignatius and it won't be about a case."

Frank smiled. "Good luck with your squash, Father."

"And your case, detective."

As Frank turned to go, he was certain a wooden box contained information he needed. He couldn't shake the priest's words about joining the border fight himself. What was underneath that rock?

Arturo tried to forget the image of Diego's wife and daughter collapsing into a wailing embrace in the doorway of their home following the detective's notice their husband and father was not just killed, but violently so. The vision hung over Arturo's interrogation of Graham Soto. He was sure Graham and Russell were blind spots for Frank.

"Russell said you usually train in groups of four or five."

Arturo studied every detail on Graham's face for a revelation.

"Yeah." Graham rubbed his large, sweaty hands against his pants. "The other guys had stuff to do that night."

"So just you and Russell."

Graham nodded, shifting around in his seat.

Arturo paused, allowing the silence to work on the boy, who continued shifting under the weight of his eyes.

"We were chasing coyote." Graham stilled, though his voice wavered.

"You hunt in the desert at night a lot?" Arturo asked.

"Maybe once a month."

It matched Russell's answer.

"And there was no one else out there that night?"

Graham shook his head.

"Why'd you join the militia?" Arturo pressed.

"I was pissed." Graham moved his gaze to a framed photo of snow-peaked mountains hanging behind the detective. "I wanted to do something about it."

"Pissed enough to want to kill?"

"No—I don't know, man." Graham shook his head, mouthing an obscenity at the floor. "My mom said if you bring me in again, she'll get an attorney."

The boy's eyes pleaded.

It was a threat on its face, but mostly it was raw meat thrown at a growling dog, out of fear, hoping to satisfy the beast. Arturo's expression softened, sympathy peeking through his eyes as he imagined the reservation attorney used often in the districts. Cheap suits and talk. "You can go, Graham."

Graham breathed out relief and a quick "bye" as he slipped out the door.

Arturo grabbed his keys and headed to his car, pulling out just behind Graham.

The old man's expression was heavy with age. He shuffled around the hogan, where he had lived alone since his wife died, with great effort, his muscles increasingly immobilized in a quicksand of time.

Frank offered a traditional Navajo greeting since Emilio's grandfather was only half Papago.

Yiska Begay was nearly a century old, still sweeping a dirt floor with a handmade flax broom. Frank was transported to an ancestral time and place he had lived through only secondhand, his grandfather's own hogan that always smelled like wet earth.

"Sit. Please." Yiska sat on a low, backless chair sipping at a handle-less clay mug of Navajo tea. With his rangy body, close-cropped white hair, jeans, and denim shirt, he looked more like an old rancher than a hundred-year-old Indian. Yiska wordlessly offered Frank a mug of tea.

Frank accepted, nearly forgetting why he had come as the first taste of greenthread herb knocked him out of the present.

"Emilio can poison an arrow, but it's only a tradition. It's a story that keeps getting told in our family. That's all."

The old man answered before Frank could ask the question. It was what the old man didn't know about his grandson that made Yiska's words untrue.

"I know he's ready to fight, but that only means he's a soldier, and not all soldiers are ready to kill," Yiska continued before Frank could speak.

"But he has to be ready to kill," Frank finally said. He understood Yiska believed the words he spoke, but they were the words of a grandfather who could only see his grandson carrying forward a tradition, not carrying out bloodthirsty passion.

"You're not convinced." Yiska smiled. "I've

heard about your case. There's no clear suspect."

Frank knew the old man was leading him around, but even in being led maybe Yiska would let something slip about Emilio. "There's no clear evidence. But when there's a soft alibi and the right passions to commit a crime, that's a kind of evidence for a man like me."

"Have you considered you are running further and further in the wrong direction, detective? Maybe you can't find your way back now," Yiska suggested.

"You do this job long enough, it happens." Frank stared into his tea, searching for wisdom from the ancient brew that might trap the old man into revealing something—just as Yiska was trying to trap him with doubt.

"The poison Emilio made—do you know what he did with it?"

"Back to the earth. He only killed a few weeds." Yiska's eyes bloomed wide with amusement.

"Did you see him dispose of his batch?"

"I saw the Sahara mustard he wilted out back. I can show you."

Frank reckoned the old man believed the mustard weed's fate was in his grandson's hands. Emilio could have simply dumped one batch as a show of good faith but made another Yiska didn't know about.

Frank shook his head. "Thank you for the tea." He stood.

"It's what I can offer. Hágoónee."

Frank echoed Yiska's Navajo goodbye, leaving the old man's seal of family loyalty intact for now.

When he wasn't coaching, Emilio spent a good deal of his time training with the militia. Frank discovered this after shadowing him for days behind binoculars. The precipitate of Frank's lurking was Father Harris, who made an appearance at the border. He proved as handy with a firearm as he was with a bow and arrow, hitting the metal guts of coffee cans with greater accuracy than some of the militia's best shooters.

At one point, Father Harris and Emilio broke away from the others, their backs barricading some intimation.

Frank rang the priest later that day. Though it felt a little superstitious, Frank sat at his desk, staring at the two arrows that killed two traffickers and hoping they would inspire the right questions of the priest.

"Father, it's Frank Silva. I noticed you made a visit to the border. Looks like you and Emilio had a lot to talk about."

There was silence after the detective's question.

"After our talk in the garden, I decided it was time to visit the border." Father Harris finally spoke. "It was my first time."

"You're a better shot than most of them—gun or arrow."

Again, silence. Conversational silences with suspects counted as responses for Frank as they were often used as an opportunity to craft just the right response. For Frank, the very existence of such silences following controversial case questions had led to arrests in the past.

"My double heritage of violence. My father taught me to hunt in the English countryside. Both of my parents were handy with a recurve."

"That night, where were you, Padre?"

"I hear Confession every Wednesday. I was in bed by midnight."

A priest in bed is expected to be alone. "Alone?"

"Yes. I'm human but that's not a weakness of mine."

Was his actual weakness the two dead traffickers? Frank let the idea play in his mind.

"I'm sorry, detective, but I'm running late for meeting someone."

Frank said "goodbye," still spinning his theory of the priest's guilt.

He had never tailed a priest. The detective followed Father Harris's red Jeep about thirty miles north of the reservation districts, exiting the highway at the town of Burning Rock.

At the town's only exit, the priest continued on for several miles, turning onto Main Street where he stopped in front of a red brick building housing with a coffee shop on the lower story. Frank hung back, pulling into a space a half block away.

Father Harris stood on the sidewalk, alternately studying a scrap of paper in his hand and searching the building's upper floor. A window opened. A woman with long, dark hair loosely tied behind her, wearing a purple sundress, waved at Father Harris. Frank squinted and Regina Acuna came into view.

So much for the rumor that Regina was living in the town of Silver.

Frank decided to wait.

The priest was upstairs for about an hour and returned alone to his car.

The detective followed Father Harris back toward the districts, all the way to the turnoff for the church, where parishioners filed in for Confession and daily evening mass.

Frank watched the lights of the church come on, wearing the many colors of stained glass.

If the priest was capable of breaking up a marriage and ignoring a vow of chastity, what else was he capable of?

·»)·✦·((·

The Martyr stared at the border, where the northern militia looked into a mirror to the south. Mothers embraced grown children. Cousins who hadn't seen one another for months touched faces and hands.

Instead of food, all varieties of firepower were brought to the reunion of north and south Tohono O'odham. Many hugged automatic rifles or pistols when they weren't embracing family.

The day was dying overhead, spilling reds and oranges across the sky. The ripples of affection within the militia finally stilled, straightening into lines of solemn expressions.

Two days before, on the outskirts of Agua Prieta, Mexico, another head appeared without its body. Like Diego Rivera, Luna Flores, a schoolteacher from Sonora, suddenly disappeared from her life.

"Heard about Luna Flores." Frank approached Emilio, who was watching the reunion at a distance.

"We're having a living memorial for Luna and Diego. We don't plan on firing these weapons today." Emilio sighed. "Yiska said you talked to him."

Of course the old man mentioned their meeting to his grandson. "You knew I would wind up in that hogan eventually."

"I figured."

The two men were silent, standing midway between breathing and inanimate memorials.

"How long will they stay?" Frank nodded at the militias.

Emilio shrugged. "We never decided officially. I'd better get back."

Frank watched Emilio return to his spot, which had remained open in his absence. It was an inconspicuous position toward the back. In fact, a much larger man eclipsed Emilio almost completely.

The sun collapsed on itself like a building on fire, leaving an ashy sky.

Frank watched the two sides watching each other, seeing the same pain reflected across the border. He tried not to feel it. He waited as they waited. Waited to solve his case. Was he waiting for more?

He walked away from his own question just as an older woman with sore feet started grumbling until her feet moved along with her lips. The others followed until only Emilio remained.

Arturo stared at the arrow on his desk, willing it to reveal who shot it into Joaquin Carrillo. His own target was becoming hazier so that he squinted even harder at it. There had been no progress beyond a weak alibi in the matter of Russell's and Graham's guilt.

Arturo returned the arrow to its evidence file and checked his phone for the time. Mid-afternoon. The high school would be letting out. He could catch Graham or Russell, or both. Arturo grabbed his keys.

Russell appeared outside the high school, but no Graham. Arturo followed Russell's silver moped for several miles to a bright, yellow brick house. Russell parked and ran inside.

About a half hour later, Russell emerged from

his front door as Arturo's eyes negotiated with his brain for a quick nap. Russell started his moped, heading back to the high school and disappearing inside. Arturo waited a moment, slipping in behind the boy.

He followed Russell to a back door propped open with a doorstop. He could see Russell standing in the archery practice yard through the cracked door but couldn't see who received the anger in his eyes.

"You shouldn't have followed me" Russell began.

"You get coach's lady pregnant? I heard she's staying in Silver."

Arturo recognized Graham's voice.

"No fuckin' way. How can you ask me that, man?"

Russell's gaze remained steady, but Arturo noticed defensiveness in his tone, which could have been disgust over an untruth against his reputation or the façade of disgust covering a lie.

Arturo thought of Frank saying the priest was capable of "dark deeds" after seeing him visit Regina at her clandestine apartment. The same could be thought of Russell if he were sneaking around with Regina. A lot of men were weak when it came to women. It didn't make them capable of murder.

Frank stood in the spot where Joaquin Carrillo and Diego Velazquez crossed over from life to death. As night swallowed a candy-colored sunset, Frank noticed a light pole brightening the clearing around the Salt Bingo casino. He wondered who would pay to keep a single light on in the middle of blank desert, next to a long-abandoned building.

The light splashed around the old casino, concentrating where the two bodies had lain. Frank noticed a wooden ladder propped horizontally against the building. He flipped the ladder, testing his weight on the first rung. It held, so he ascended to the roof, which was doused in enough light for Frank to notice a perfect vantage point for an arrow shot.

He knelt down, the crackling of his arthritic knees reminding him of his ex-wife and twin daughters nagging him to exercise, eat better, and retire. The first two were considerations. The latter he dreaded.

Frank nodded to himself that an accurate aim was possible with the light of the pole lamp. He looked around the roof. Though there was no evidence of a murderous archer, the roof was an ideal vantage point. Frank stared at the lamp, which drew him back toward the clearing. It just happened to shine right on the spot where two men were cut down with arrows. A shooter would have had to know when the traffickers would pass under the light. It seemed strange for someone to pay to keep the light on when there was nothing but blank desert for miles in every direction.

Even if the traffickers had traveled a regular route, someone would have had to observe them at night—someone who had just lost his wife to another man and balanced precariously on his emotions. Someone who couldn't care less about eight pounds of heroin stashed on a couple of traffickers.

The brushy ground seemed to whisper to Frank, Emilio, Emilio, Emilio.

Frank mashed two words he read in a property assessment document together in his brain until he remembered why he recognized them. Carlos Rios was the name of the owner of the casino. At least it was the name of the limited liability corporation that had recently purchased it, which could be one person or a thousand.

"Is this the name of the owner in the file?" Frank tapped a plastic window to get a county assessment worker's attention. The worker shook her head.

Frank looked up Carlos Rios, the LLC, on his phone. There was nothing listed so he referenced the man behind the name. For this knowledge, he didn't need his phone. For those Tohono O'odham who knew their people's history, Rios was a notable war chief in the early twentieth century, and for the past few months a business with the same name chose to buy a forgotten casino, even paying to keep a single light pole on next to it without making any changes to the land or the building on it. Maybe the company was moving slowly with its plans for profiting off the casino, or maybe something else was happening in a nowhere patch of desert.

"What about the former owner?" Frank persisted.

The clerk began typing, pulling the name Orrin Campillo. He lived in the Natchez District, a district Frank wasn't so familiar with. Natchez was at the other end of the reservation, a polarity to Rainmaker, where much of the reservation population was concentrated. Frank hoped Mr. Campillo would be easy to find, and he hoped he could tell him something about Carlos Rios, the business.

A young woman was on the other side of Frank's knock. "I'm looking for an Orrin Campillo." Frank held up his badge.

The woman squinted at it. "He passed away several months ago. I'm his daughter. Can I help?"

"Maybe. Orrin sold the casino to someone and I'm trying to figure out who."

The woman shook her head, looking away. "I wouldn't know." She turned her wet eyes on Frank. "We weren't really talking right before he died." She wiped her eyes on her index finger. "Anyway, the only person who might know is my uncle, and he disappeared right after my father died. He was a silent partner in the casino."

Of course, another cul-de-sac. "What's his name?"

"Martin Campillo."

"Any idea where he might be?"

The woman shrugged, then frowned. "He goes to Mexico a lot."

"For what?"

More shrugging.

"If you find out where your uncle went . . ." Frank handed over his card.

"Does this have anything to do with those murders?"

"I hope so," he mumbled to himself, throwing more cordial words back at the woman as he walked away.

CHAPTER
2

Even though the night was already starting to blind him, Arturo followed Russell at a distance, allowing other cars to sandwich between as a buffer. Russell moved off the main highway to a secondary route that ended at a darkened St. Ignatius. A light switched on at the rectory as soon as Father Harris appeared in the doorway. Russell disappeared with the light behind the closed door.

Was Russell Catholic? Most of the kids in the district didn't practice anything other than some scratching around in indigenous spirituality that didn't amount to much more than an abuse of peyote.

Arturo turned off his car, waiting about ten minutes before Russell appeared. If Russell was Catholic and confessing to a mortal sin, the meeting would have lasted longer. There was the odd triangulation of Russell, the priest, and Emilio's ex-wife, which was irrelevant to the case, but might explain Russell meeting with Father Harris.

Arturo watched the light of Russell's motorbike disappear as the boy drove away from the church, then pulled out his phone, dialing. "Anything on Campillo?"

"Maybe," Frank answered.

"What?"Arturo asked impatiently, switching on his car's ignition.

"Have you heard of a Martin Campillo?" Frank asked.

"Nope."

"He's Orrin's brother and owned half the casino.

His niece says he might know who bought it. She said he might be in Mexico, but she couldn't say where."

"So it's a dead end?" Arturo asked, annoyed by yet another weak lead.

Frank sighed. "Maybe, or not."

"What's the 'maybe not'?" Pushing down harder on the gas pedal, Arturo released frustration over the slow-progressing case in a burst of speed.

"There's an Indian I know down in Hermosillo. He's reliable. He can probably find Campillo."

"What's his price?" Arturo let the blank, dark desert, broken only by an occasional patch of distant light, hypnotize him away from the case for a moment.

"He owes me a big favor, so probably nothing."

"Speaking of dead ends, Russell just left a private meeting with the priest."

"Maybe the kid got religion." Frank cleared a chuckle from his throat.

"I don't know. He had an argument with Graham. Said he shouldn't have followed him. Seems strange he would go straight to the priest right after."

"That's what Catholics do. They have a problem, they see their priest."

"You're the one who said the priest had a dark side. If the kid went to see him, maybe they both know something."

Frank was silent.

"Just seems like we're putting more live bodies in between us and the dead ones." Again, Arturo pressed his gas pedal for another feeling of release.

"Sometimes you have to drift awhile before you hit land."

"Maybe." Arturo was tired of drifting. "Keep me posted on Campillo."

Arturo hung up and headed straight home. He didn't even feel like a drive by Russell's house to make sure he was there for the night.

·》》》·✦·《《《·

Frank had been across the border many times to visit cousins and aunts and uncles on his mother's side of the family in Magdalena de Kino. Like a rubber band, the Tohono O'odham of Arizona stretched into Sonora, Mexico, through families who had once come and gone seamlessly across the border.

Mexico was not another country for Frank. It wasn't even another state. Maybe it was becoming that way, Frank thought as he waited while a border guard studied his badge and ID. The guard finally passed him through after Frank answered questions he had never heard asked at the border before: "Where are you headed?" "Are you here on business?" "Is this your first time in Mexico?" "Do you have family you're visiting?"

He noticed a few solemn faces on either side, impressed they had sustained the fervor of the first memorial he had witnessed. The gap between the mirroring lines of remembrance had widened, no doubt due to the increased security. Instead of the single guard, there were three, each housed in a crude shed, while construction on permanent security booths went on next to their temporary twins.

Frank thought he saw an angry expression on one of the solemn women standing south of the border. She aimed her anger at one of the new guards.

As he left the anger and tension at the border behind him, Frank read a note he had made in his phone. Martin Campillo was staying in La Colorada. Frank's connection in Hermosillo had come through. The remote town was an odd choice for a greedy businessman, unless he was hiding out there. La Colorada was a pinprick of a pueblo in the state of Sonora.

Several hours deep into Sonora, Frank finally arrived at the old mining village, tucked into the foothills of the Sierra Madre Occidental Range, where a scattering of adobe homes and businesses crept up the base of a foothill like a permanent wave.

Driving past the heart of the town, Frank reached a cluster of trailer homes. He passed the trailers and rounded a foothill where he discovered more adobe houses. Frank slowed down at a salmon-colored residence, then continued on, parking in a gravel alley a few blocks away and starting on foot toward the pink house.

There was an old green pickup parked in the driveway, which Frank's contact said would be there. Frank knocked on the door once, then twice. The door opened wide enough for a dark eye to notice Frank's badge before it disappeared. As soon as Frank heard running feet against the entryway floor, he ran as fast as his arthritic knees would allow, toward the back of the house where Martin Campillo wasn't moving much quicker down a brushy incline. Frank was used to the chase, though, working with gravity instead of fighting it. He made up the gap with this speed, colliding with the other man at the bottom of the incline.

Pinning the man with his weight, Frank managed to restrain his arms against the ground.

"You bastards don't have anything on me." Martin grunted, pushing up fruitlessly against Frank, who was the larger man.

"Maybe we do," Frank said blankly, unsure about the man's actual crimes. Martin Campillo had obviously anticipated a confrontation with authorities, or he wouldn't have run.

Martin spit at Frank. "Fuck you." He struggled underneath, nearly knocking Frank off.

Frank decided to aim more specifically. "We can connect your casino."

"I can't help those fuckers passing my building. You aren't gonna find shit."

Frank realized Martin was talking about traffickers using his casino as a meetup or maybe even distribution site. It made sense. It was isolated, perfect for shadowy activity. If Martin was money hungry like his niece said, the cartel would have paid him well to use his empty casino north of the border.

Martin kneed Frank in the groin. Frank released Martin's wrists as his hands moved protectively toward the pain. The other man ran off without any regard for gravity this time. Frank grimaced at the remaining discomfort between his legs but managed to get to his feet. He started running but had already lost Martin. Frank could wait him out, but men like Martin had back-up plans for such dilemmas—he could be in Singapore by the end of the day. Frank drove back through the center of La Colorada, tracing its grid of crumbly alleys and side streets, but as he suspected, the other man had vanished.

He returned to his car, settling in for several hours of watching Martin's house. At the very least, he would return to the desert with a warrant to kick in the door of the Salt Bingo.

Arturo watched Russell scouring the ground around the Salt Bingo. After giving the boy a head start, he crouched behind a boulder, following Russell through binoculars toward the casino. Though he carried his bow, Russell mostly scanned the ground immediately around him as if he had lost something. He was near the crime scene but never reached it with his feet or his eyes.

At one point, Arturo noticed Russell take aim and shoot some sort of varmint, tossing it in a sack slung across his back after removing the arrow from the creature's twitching body, even as his eyes continued their sweep of ground. The killing of the varmint was too reflexively accurate.

Russell stooped down to examine something. Arturo squinted through his binoculars. It looked like a hop bush. The boy studied the shrub for a moment, then kept moving. He repeated this process several times over an hour, stooping and investigating shrubs.

If he was guilty, why wasn't he studying the murder scene? Was there something out there he thought would convict him? If Russell was that worried about being discovered, why would he have left the two bodies in an open clearing to begin with?

On the other hand, why snoop around in a crime scene if you didn't have something to gain? Arturo circled back to his suspicion, waiting until Russell returned to his moped before retracing the boy's steps. There was nothing unusual—only empty beer bottles and scattered trash here and there.

Arturo stood staring at the Salt Bingo and the crime scene, imagining arrows flying from where he stood. A clear shot. He pulled an invisible nocking point back toward his cheek, once, then twice, nodding to himself. It bothered Arturo, though, that Russell would just be scouring the area around a murder for a possibly damning piece of evidence. If the hypothetical piece of evidence was substantial enough to come back for, why wasn't it still there? Was it valuable or valuable through blackmail?

Above this question, two others pecked holes in Russell as a suspect. How could the kid have known the poison would take down a man instantly, and how could he have known when the traffickers would pass by? It seemed like a lot for a Rez kid to manage, and Frank's words about not risking a full ride out of Rainmaker haunted Arturo. He had dug a hole around the kid that was filling up with as much doubt as guilt.

·)))·✦·(((·

Frank wasn't surprised at how easily he secured a warrant to enter the Salt Bingo. Not only was he a friend, but this particular judge loathed the cartel and anyone tied to them. It didn't hurt that Frank had hit "record" on his phone as soon as Martin Campillo answered his door.

"You want to do the honors?" Frank motioned toward the casino's padlock with a bolt cutter.

"It's your warrant." Arturo nodded back at the padlock.

"Okay, here we go." Frank tossed the lock on the ground and pushed the door open with his foot.

Darkness swept back out what little light the detectives flushed in as the heavy metal door to the main entrance slammed shut behind the men. Frank sniffed deeply at a musty mixture with notes of body odor, urine and beer biting through the air.

Arturo switched on a flashlight.

"Looks like someone cleaned up," Frank noticed a concrete floor stamped by at least fifty outlines of slot machines and craps and blackjack tables. Off to the side, a row of cages still stood where winners and losers no doubt cashed out through the plastic windows. "Other than the smell." Frank whistled his judgment.

"Looks like someone really cleaned up," Arturo said, throwing light everywhere.

Arturo slowed his beam, focusing it on the smooth floor of the single-room casino, exposing two bathrooms stripped down to metal piping, and presumably an office and maintenance closet. Orange paint lifted away from the concrete in many areas, further revealing neglect.

"Pretty slim operation," Arturo remarked, pushing at a particularly rebellious curl of paint with his toe.

"Gamblers don't need many comforts to part with their money." Frank noticed a large crack in the floor. He stooped down. "Gimme some light over here." Frank crouched down carefully on his arthritic knees, grimacing despite this precaution. There were cracks branching across the floor, but the fracture Frank targeted was by far the widest and longest.

Arturo spotlighted a wide radius around Frank, who probed the spot in question with his index finger.

"There's something here." Frank picked at something thin and cylindrical with a gloved hand. "Dammit." Frank's scowl lit up with a boogeyman's glow in Arturo's light. "Jammed in there."

"Here try this." Arturo handed Frank a pocketknife.

Leveraging the blade, Frank pushed up at different points along the object until it popped out of the crack. Frank held out an arrow.

"Is that the same?" Arturo asked, nodding his light at the arrow. "It sure looks the same."

Frank rolled the wood between thumb and index finger, squinting, although he didn't need to squint. He squinted because he couldn't believe what he saw at first glance. It was the same material and design as the two poisoned arrows that killed two men right outside the casino. "If someone else bought this place from Campillo, and that someone is our suspect, it makes sense for it to be stripped down. They keep it the way Campillo left it so the cartel won't pick up that they bought it. Maybe." Frank marveled at the possibility of the leap that he was holding an arrow that belonged to the suspect.

"Why hide it here? This one thing?" Arturo asked. "Russell was out here looking for something. Maybe this?"

"Could be." Frank stared at the arrow as if he could release its mystery this way. "If Russell is our guy, then maybe the cartel put this here." Frank spoke to the arrow. "But why? It wasn't exactly easy for us to find, and if they want to take Russell down, why not just take his head?"

"Maybe we'll get lucky with prints on this one," Arturo suggested.

"Wouldn't bet on it even in this place." Frank opened his mouth to say more, but his eyes widened at something. "Look at this." He pointed at the fletching, holding in his next breath. "It's like a puzzle piece. See the blue here? The same blue is in the other arrows. This blue suddenly stops here and does the same thing on one of the other two arrows, but on the third arrow it cuts through the red across the entire arrow. We need to get this pattern in front of someone who can interpret it."

If no one else would, maybe it was time for the arrows to talk.

Dr. Rex Sells touched the arrows only with his dark eyes at first, finally elevating one on gloved palms toward a bright light. "I've seen these before." His lids inflated and deflated as he studied the arrows from different angles.

Frank and Arturo glanced at one another.

"They were on display at the Desert People Museum," the archeology professor asserted. "Belonged to a Papago chief."

"Is the chief Carlos Rios, by any chance?" Frank asked.

"Actually, it is. I didn't know you were so up on our tribal history, Frank." Dr. Sells smiled.

"No better than I was in school. Just fits with what we already know."

"You happen to know what these fletching markings mean?" Arturo asked.

Dr. Sells shook his head. "There are maybe thousands of distinctive fletching markings, and I only know about a hundred."

"You think these were stolen since they were in a museum?" Frank asked.

"Could be. It didn't get a lot of traffic. Probably why it closed. Only visitors were artifact junkies like me."

"Who ran the museum?" Arturo asked.

"Actually, it was privately run by a man named Jessie Topawa. If I remember right, he lived over in Coyote District."

"Then that's where we're headed." Frank hoped Jessie Topawa was easier to track down than Martin Campillo.

"This is only about a quarter of what we had at the museum." Jessie Topawa nodded panoramically around his trailer that contained everything from animal-bone weapons to earthenware bowls decorated with patterns and colors reflecting several tribes.

Frank nodded. "They take anything else?"

"Just these." Jessie nodded at the arrows. "I filed a police report, but honestly, it was partly my fault because I forgot to lock a window that night and the thief crawled right in. We never had a camera either."

"How long ago?" Frank asked.

"About a month."

"If this isn't our guy, this is the guy that sold to our guy. You think someone would sell these at a pawn shop, or maybe online?" Frank hovered a hand over the arrows.

"Pawn shops around here wouldn't know how to price something like this, so they'd probably pass, but you never can tell. I'd say online, but that's a black hole. I wouldn't know where to send you first." Jessie's eyes lit up. "I know a guy who sells this kind of thing. He might be able to get you started."

Frank collected the name and Arturo the arrows. He only hoped the arrows were leading in the right direction.

·))) · ✦ · (((·

Frank raised his brows at the trio of arrows as if they had told him the protective finish on their wood bodies was only a couple of months old. Ray Hernandez, an expert in ancient Native American weaponry, followed up his age estimate with two words: Sun Blush.

"Huh?" Arturo asked.

"A plant with pink flowers, right?" Frank added.

Ray nodded. "When the flowers bloom, you can excise a liquid that's a main ingredient in the wood protectant." Ray hovered a hand just over the arrows. "Pretty old technique too."

"Belonged to Carlos Rios," Frank mentioned.

"Rios used Wood Blood—that's what they used to call it," Ray said. "No one uses it anymore."

"Why would someone use it?" Arturo asked.

Ray shrugged. "No reason to. Plenty of synthetic options out there that work just as well or better."

Old ways with new purpose pointed back at Emilio. Time for another visit to Yiska's hogan.

The half Navajo stood motionless behind his mud-sealed shack. Frank watched him taking in sunset embers.

"It's my favorite time of the day," Yiska said.

Acknowledgment of his presence interrupted Frank's gaze, which shifted back to why he came. "Sometimes I see it through my office window."

"Not the same thing, though." Yiska smiled mostly through his eyes.

"No," Frank agreed. "You ever hear of Wood Blood?"

Yiska lingered in a new smile. "You don't waste time even for a sunset, detective. My grandfather used it, and I'm sure you want to know that he taught me how to make it, but that I never passed it on to Emilio."

Frank would have been annoyed with a younger man, but Yiska drew on the privilege of age.

"Is it easy to make?"

"It was easy when we lived closer to all of this a hundred years ago." Yiska swept a hand across the desert. "Now, it's not so simple."

"You ever make it?" Frank asked.

Yiska shook his head. "Not these days. My arrows are long retired, anyway."

"Anyone you know make it or sell it?"

Yiska shook his head again. "If someone is selling it, I don't know about it. In my day we made it. We didn't sell it." Yiska paused.

The two men stood silently for a moment before Frank left with Yiska's words reverberating inside. It wasn't the words about the Wood Blood that carried so much weight, but those about living so far from earth and sky, the places that once defined the Tohono O'odham—the Papago. He tried shaking off the reflection as a natural symptom of his age. Instead, it swelled with thoughts of Emilio and his militia defending a border that was the last, weakest battleground of a forgotten war. All for a way of life preserved in the sunset memories of a handful of old men and women.

CHAPTER
3

Through binoculars, Arturo closed his distance with Russell, who once again hunted for something too close to the site of the murders.

Russell flinched almost imperceptibly, his heightened muscular responses no doubt earned through many hours of tracking game.

"I know this looks bad," Russell began.

"It doesn't look good," Arturo continued.

"How good would it look if you found the arrowhead I lost? I know it was stone heads that killed those two," Russell retorted.

Arturo shrugged. "But I caught you out here, anyway. You gambled coming back twice, which means there's a good chance you're worried about someone finding what you lost. And you're the only one I've seen around here looking for anything." Arturo watched the thought sink in, hoping to surface a twitch of guilt somewhere. Russell gave up nothing, his gaze unchanged, steady on Arturo.

"I'm the only one out here because I'm the only one who hunts with stone. Graham and the other guys use steel heads." Russell remained perfectly still, other than his right hand tugging at a leather strap crossing his body and securing a quiver at his back.

As he explained, Russell's eyes remained anchored on the detective.

"But that's the problem right there. You laid it bare." Arturo rubbed off a layer of sandy ground with the toe of his boot, illustrating his point.

"But I'm being straight with you, man. I'm out here because I don't have anything to hide. Wouldn't you do the same?"

"That's not how this works. You have to put yourself in my shoes. You can't afford not to." Arturo waited again for his words to take effect in the boy, but there was stillness in Russell, like ice trapping all sound and motion over a lake. Arturo recognized it as the practiced pose of a predator in the presence of game.

"What about my shoes?" Only Russell's lips moved.

"I have to balance your shoes with my case." Arturo searched for any weak spot in Russell's demeanor, but there wasn't so much as a flaring nostril.

"Why do you hunt out here?"

"There's good skunk pig hunting out here. And, there's that light." Russell nodded at the pole. "There ain't shit out here otherwise, so it's just easy to meet by the old casino."

It made sense.

"You ever see anything strange out here around the casino?"

Russell broke the ice over his expression with a small grin. "You mean like mules passing through?"

"Yeah, like that." Arturo frowned. "Or anyone or anything that doesn't belong."

Russell shook his head, lips flatlining back to serious.

"What about you and the coach's lady?" Arturo held in his own grin. He wanted to keep the boy talking as long as he could for a deeper study of his responses.

Russell remained still, other than a small parting of his lips releasing more than breath. It was the kind of detail the detective couldn't help but collect.

"How do you know—" Russell began, but closed his mouth over the rest of his question.

"I saw you and Graham arguing." Arturo watched Russell's expression for even subtle evidence of new panic.

Russell looked at the ground, searching for something other than an arrowhead. "What does that have to do with anything, man?"

"Well, if something is going on between you

and Regina, that would say something about your character, wouldn't it? And if you can't be trusted to not sleep with your coach's wife, then maybe I can't trust what you're saying about why you're out here looking for an arrowhead."

"It would if something actually happened." Russell blew deep breaths through his nose.

"Why did Graham think there was something going on?"

Russell looked at the ground again, his eyes roving. "I stayed with them for a while. Things were bad at my house."

Arturo believed the boy. Russell's father was a drunk and a mean one. Arturo's mother had abandoned Russell and his father after too many visits from Rez police following alcohol-fueled fights between the boy's parents.

"So where did Graham follow you?"

"To Silver. I thought that's where Regina went. There's like ninety people there, so I thought I could ask around about her."

"Why would he think you were going there, and why were you looking for her?" Arturo knew it wasn't a loose thread directly attached to the case, but it was a loose thread in a suspect's life, and that made it an important thread to pull.

"It was kind of a coincidence. We were gonna practice bag shooting at the school, and I told him I had to clean out the garage with my dad instead. Graham came over to borrow my bag because his is a piece of shit. My dad was lit and told Graham I was probably out lookin' for that bitch. And coach told us he thought she was in Silver, so Graham caught up to me. He was pissed that I blew him off for a woman and wanted me to know. Didn't find her anyway." Russell sighed, looking away before answering the second question. "She's like my mom." Russell's icy pose melted, his shoulders slumping.

Arturo realized the boy felt abandoned by a mother for the second time in his life. Obviously, Regina didn't want to be found. He couldn't bring himself to tell the boy about the priest visiting Regina's apartment in Burning Rock.

"Okay, why don't I help you look for your arrowhead," Arturo offered out of sympathy but also as a test. If Russell declined his assistance, it would be suspicious.

Russell nodded.

Arturo and Russell searched in silence for the arrowhead. The detective spent as much time watching Russell's movements as he did looking for a flaked piece of stone that still hadn't turned up after an hour. Arturo agreed to call off the search, wondering if, like Russell, he was looking too hard for something that just wasn't there.

•))) · ✦ · (((•

Frank stood at a distance from the San Felipe Gate, watching a silent movie play out. He could see

Emilio on his knees, hands cuffed behind him, lips animated in the direction of a white man in bullet-proof black standing over him. Another man dressed in a dark green uniform was on his knees and remained very still, even though Emilio alternated between sending his anger at the white man and the man in green. Frank had often approached crime scenes this way, quietly shadowing the language of faces and bodies. This wasn't his crime scene, though. He was a secondary player, piggybacking with his own case, hoping for a few minutes with the accused.

"Detective Silva with the county." Frank held up his badge for the black-vested man as he entered the crime scene, catching Emilio's eyes that seemed to plead with Frank.

"You're on that murder case," the other man said.

Frank was surprised at the rapid travel of news through the veins of Homeland Security. He nodded, then looked toward Emilio. "I need a minute with him." Frank glanced quickly at the other kneeling man, who he noticed was also Tohono O'odham. "What happened here?" he asked before the federal agent could say 'yay' or 'nay' to his request.

The agent stepped away from Emilio, pulling Frank closer with his eyes. "That one"—the agent pointed at the kneeling border guard—"was paid off by someone, no doubt cartel, to start something with the other one." The agent eyed Emilio.

"Looks like it got physical," Frank observed,

noticing a patch of dried blood near the corner of Emilio's mouth.

"Another guard broke it up before it went further."

"Can you give me a minute with Emilio Acuna?"

"Make it quick. He needs to be processed."

Frank returned to Emilio, who glared at the kneeling guard while he stared blankly out at the desert.

"What did he say?" Frank sank down on bent knees meeting Emilio eye-to-eye, intentionally obscuring the younger man's line of sight with his fresh enemy. He winced inwardly as the pain stabbed at the nerves in his knee.

"He's a turncoat. That's all you need to know," Emilio retorted.

Confusion in Frank's eyes asked his next question.

"Bastard was paid off by the cartel."

"To do what?"

"To piss us off—to get us hot. He was yelling all kinds of bullshit at us, talking about Diego and Luna."

Frank noticed a half wreath of militia members spectating quietly or in low voices. "To piss you off," Frank added. "You're the only one in handcuffs. Or maybe it doesn't take much to get you going these days."

"This is perfect for you, isn't it?" Emilio shook his head, glaring at the turncoat. "Look at that asshole. He can't even look at me or you or anyone. He's dead inside."

Emilio's last comment stunned Frank for a moment. Like Yiska's reflection at the hogan, Emilio's words unsettled the detective. "Where do you think all of this is headed?" Frank asked.

Emilio slumped forward a little, sighing. "More of this." He nodded at the other kneeling man.

"Then what's the point of training the militia so hard?"

Emilio straightened. "We want strength. We need to be strong, even if we only use our strength to keep our kids from becoming mules or to keep them off the drugs dropped on our Rez."

"You sound like a revolutionary," Frank observed. "And a lot of revolutions have started with a single assassination or murder."

"Sounds like an accusation."

Frank shrugged. "In my line of work most things sound like accusations to the guilty."

"We've been here a few times already. You've got no hard evidence on me. Just speculation." Emilio looked up at Frank.

Frank had to admit that Emilio was a man of integrity and always spoke straight. Even now, there was no hesitation or holding back in the younger man's gaze, but he could only compartmentalize this personal bias.

Frank breathed in, releasing a sigh. "You know anything about Wood Blood?"

Emilio licked the dried blood at the corner of his lip. "I've heard my grandfather mention it, but I wouldn't know how to make it, which is what you really want to know."

"So he doesn't make it or sell it?" Frank knew he was darkening a line already drawn by Yiska, but it was a useful tool in detective work. Truth had to echo through everyone it touched. If it didn't, it wasn't truth. It was fragmented somewhere by a lie or doubt.

Emilio shook his head but stopped mid-shake, looking up at the detective, interrogating with his eyes. Frank answered unwillingly from inside his conscience. "You think I'm a traitor too. A traitor to my people."

Frank pushed back with his own eyes.

"You're staring so hard at one thing you don't want to look at anything else." Emilio shifted his weight from one bent leg to the other.

"Anyone else you mean," Frank retorted.

"Maybe, but I think I represent your idea of what the killer should look like. And it's easy for you to see my anger everywhere. You see it in all these faces." Emilio nodded at the other militia members. "You're trying too hard to be objective and textbook. But you can't because maybe you're as pissed off as we are, but you're not letting yourself feel it, so you're not seeing the truth. Accusing me is a way to hide from the truth."

Even before Emilio finished talking, Frank's brain told him his suspect was creating a weak distraction, but Emilio's theory was a fog that settled inside Frank and wouldn't lift, so he pushed around it temporarily.

"Looks like we're at an impasse then," Frank said.

"Guess so," Emilio replied.

Frank noticed the younger man's tired eyes. They

looked out at the nothingness of the desert, but Frank sensed they saw more, reaching beyond the moment.

Frank found The Martyr's blank expression. He wanted to punch both unfeeling eyes.

It was an impulse he hadn't had in years. Violence in his line of work had become almost methodical. Physical aggression had become a deliberated, calculated answer at the end of a mathematical formula, but the younger man had insulted Frank, insinuating the detective was hiding some righteous anger behind a badge. It was a badge that had helped Frank protect his homeland and the people in it for many years. Why did it bother him that Emilio was questioning that truth?

Frank left Emilio to the desert without a "goodbye."

Frank stared at a memory inside of a frame on his mantel: His ex-wife, Mina, with her dark hair piled in a loose bun and eyes that searched Frank through the frame. The twins stood on either side of Mina, sharing Frank's wide cheekbones bridged by their mother's long, elegant nose. It all broke through to the present, questioning Frank more than Emilio.

They were all scattered like seeds on the wind, growing in separate directions. Allegra was pre-med on the East Coast, and Maron guided raft trips in the

Pacific Northwest. Mina was in Santa Fe painting the land and sky. He spoke to the girls only a couple of times a month and Mina much less frequently.

Even at a distance, they were a chorus in his ears asking him what was stopping him from solving his case. It was a question his wife and daughters had often asked when they all lived in the same house. With few exceptions the question had always jarred something loose, a deep down below the surface detail, and Frank had been able to discover something overlooked that he could turn into forward momentum.

This time, though, the question budged nothing. It sat unanswered atop the pile of questions about Emilio and Yiska and Wood Blood, and smaller questions about Graham and Russell that were already beginning to decay in value. Amid all of these questions was one that stood out even more so than his wife's and daughters'. Was he as angry as Emilio about the traffickers, about what they had taken from his people, and what they would keep taking? The question stood separate from the pile, but Frank didn't want to answer it. So he grabbed his keys instead.

Frank and Arturo stared down at the clearing from the top of the former casino's roof.

"How do you practice taking down a man with a poisoned arrow?" Frank asked. "These things are precise. You need live targets."

"Javelina aren't near big enough," Arturo observed.

"And how did our guy know they were coming through here like a train pulling into a station?"

"Someone would have to see a pattern or get tipped off," Arturo said.

Frank nodded. "A pattern," he repeated. "What?" Arturo asked.

"Carlos Rios. Why was it his symbol on the arrow fletching and on the paperwork for this building?"

Arturo nodded, then shrugged. "Could be another dead end. Now there's a pattern." The younger detective snorted lightly.

"Smart ass." Frank shook his head. "We need something to bite on."

And this is all we've got, Frank said to the clearing.

The man who took the life of Carlos Rios also died at the hand of his victim. An Apache warrior, Rios's assassin entered battle singularly targeting Rios amidst the violent chaos. He was a surgical killer— the kind that Frank and Arturo hunted. He had taken down Rios with a single, poisoned arrow. Right before he died, Rios reciprocated with his own shot into the enemy's gut. In the life and death of Carlos Rios, two things stood out to Frank: First, in 1901, Rios and around twenty Papago warriors defeated nearly one hundred Mexican soldiers in a border battle for a small pocket of reservation land. Second, one of the memorials dedicated to Rios still stood not far from the Salt Bingo.

Frank returned once more to the peripheral belt of reservation land, discovering Rios's memorial about 400 feet east of the casino. Colorful offerings of dried flowers, tied together with ribbon or twine weighted under rocks, lay at all angles around the memorial, which was no more than a smooth quartzite stone inscribed with the words Carlos Rios Chief of the Papago. Besides the flowers, there wasn't much, except for the remains of a broken piece of pottery, a piece of leather that was unrecognizable from its original intended purpose, and trash— mostly empty whiskey bottles and cigarette butts. Anything of value would have already been stolen.

What caught Frank's attention wasn't the memorial, but a rough footpath that ran away from it in the direction of the Salt Bingo. Frank followed the path all the way back to the casino's overgrown parking lot. He guessed memorial visitors had used the casino as a starting point when seeking out Rios's shrine in the empty desert.

Frank had dismissed this path in his initial assessment of the crime scene. He had seen it but was well aware that traffickers like Joaquin and Diego had been conditioned to leave no trace of their presence north of the border, going so far as to vary their routes. This path too was littered with trash, particularly beer cans and broken glass. Frank noticed a couple of smaller, short branch paths cut away to clusters of cacti and rocks where an overabundance of cactus "pup" blooms offered evidence of drunken urination.

This wasn't a mule's footpath. Local feet made this trail and used it. On the other hand, the traffickers could be using the local's route to hide their tracks in plain sight under a continuous flow of foot traffic. The path would take a mule further away from civilization, but what's 400 hundred feet out of the way when you could add another layer of insurance to your strategy?

Then there was the Carlos Rios pattern. The name was associated with the murder weapon and the building standing next to the killing site. Frank crept slowly back toward the memorial, cataloging everything that fell on or along the perimeters of the path. He couldn't help notice the Sun Blush flowers growing in clusters here and there, reminding him of the Wood Blood and Rios. Next to one of these clusters was a Cow's Tongue Prickly Pear Plant that had been flattened by something heavy, and there was dried blood inking a few of the needles. Frank's first theory was a drunk had passed out, but then he noticed battered Blue Yucca and Spanish Bayonet plants next to the bloodied prickly pear as if someone had not simply passed out but had struggled in some way.

Frank swiveled toward the other side of the

path, looking for parallel destruction. Another bayonet plant was mortally deformed. He searched for similar damage elsewhere along the path, confirming the violence done to the prickly pear and neighboring plants was exceptional.

Frank pulled out his phone, dialing the records department back at headquarters. "Any assaults called in near the old Salt Bingo recently?"

It was a flat "no."

"What about the past year?" Frank persisted.

The response was another negative.

Frank returned to his car, retrieving a plastic bag and gloves. As he sealed up the bag of needles, Frank looked back at the casino. He considered the response from the records department, which loosened a memory of the sharp decline of criminal behavior at the closing of the Salt Bingo a few years back. Even amidst the reflective solemnity of a pilgrim's path, there was bound to be an altercation now and again with alcoholism poisoning the blood of so many born on The Rez. It was the nature of The Rez. On the other hand, an unreported confrontation so close to a murder site couldn't be underestimated.

Frank delivered the needles to the lab at headquarters, watching the lab door from his desk.

"Jorge Mercado," the tech announced. "Must not be so great at what he does. He's in the system for trafficking in New Mexico and Colorado, so he's been picked up a few times but never here."

"Is he held anywhere now?"

The tech shook his head.

"Is he with Caballo Negro?"

The tech nodded.

"What about the age of the blood?

"About five months old."

Frank did the quick math of the age of the blood versus the date of the murders outside the Salt Bingo, nodding to himself into his next question. "Any link to Carrillo or Velazquez?"

The tech shook his head again.

Nodding thanks, Frank's thoughts were already back on the footpath near the Salt Bingo. He had been right about the traffickers hiding in plain sight. Mercado and the two victims belonged to the same cartel. Did Mercado encounter the person who killed Joaquin and Diego, but manage to get away? It was a faint connection since the violence done to Mercado appeared to be spontaneous, whereas there was a calculated precision of the highest degree behind the arrows that struck Joaquin and Diego. On the other hand, the confrontation with Mercado could have been the precursor to poisoned arrowheads.

Frank headed back to his car, following his thoughts back to the Salt Bingo. He walked his eyes more slowly over the damaged plants, the lipstick pink of nearby Sun Blush blooms drawing his attention, one of them holding it.

The plant's five blooms had crumpled at some

point under the weight of an unnatural death delivered through a small incision. "Wood Blood," Frank whispered, separating the plant from its roots with a pocketknife. He checked other Sun Blush plants at least fifteen feet in both directions, but all other blooms were lushly filled out, and no additional excisions had been made.

The trafficker's blood was found just several feet from the excision. Coincidence? Or not? Did the same person who killed Joaquin and Diego cut into the Sun Blush to make the Wood Blood? Was there a vigilante attacking traffickers? It was a bit of a leap.

Frank stared at the bagged plant, thinking of the black hole he was digging for the case and himself, with each new discovery dying on impact with the case. He was missing something. Overlooking some critical detail, but he couldn't tap into whatever it was.

Frank studied the sliced plant flesh, exhausted of its viscous treasure. He wondered about other uses for Sun Blush. Retrieving his phone, he found nothing online other than a few men on an erectile dysfunction forum talking about applying a drop of the excised liquid to their privates for increased virility. Other than this outlier, there was only the use already familiar to Frank. He wondered if the one plant was enough for three arrows. He pulled up the recipe on his phone, noticing something else sticking out like a crooked finger. Cow hoof powder. Frank had heard of it somewhere. Where? His grandmother had used it for something when Frank was a child. He couldn't remember what, but what he did remember was how difficult it was for her to obtain even back in those days.

Frank searched online for cow hoof powder, but there were only questions without answers on an archery forum. It was back to the old half Navajo.

"Yá'át'ééh."

Frank heard the Navajo "hello" before he saw the man who spoke it. The greeting carried Frank behind the hogan, where Yiska pondered a raised garden bed, his back to the detective.

"Guess that's the beauty of living out here. You hear every engine." Frank hoped he was right about hearing every engine, and he wasn't about to give an old man a scare.

Yiska didn't jump, but he was still and silent for a moment as if Frank hadn't spoken at all.

"Never knew radishes could grow in this soil." Frank approached closer, wondering if the old man hadn't heard him.

"The soil in the bed is different than the ground around it. Emilio told me what he said to you," Yiska responded at last.

Now it was Frank who was quiet, his brain restarted from its original purpose in coming to see

Yiska. "I've always been proud of where I come from. It's why I became a detective. To protect this place and these people." He felt the passion of his own words as if he were listening instead of speaking.

"You're defending yourself, but I haven't accused you of anything," Yiska said.

"Emilio did it for you," Frank retorted.

"Maybe he was trying to wake you up."

"I'm not asleep to what's happening. I'm just doing my job. Which is why I'm here."

"Why else would you be here?" Yiska smiled through his eyes while his lips remained a still, straight line.

Frank ignored his temerity. "You know anything about cow hoof powder?"

"I know enough to know no one uses it anymore."

"Do you know where to get it?" Frank asked.

Yiska squinted at the answer. "There's a woman like me—half Navajo—who sells it out of her hogan. She lives further out than I do. Her hogan is alone off Route 44 where it cuts off onto 27. You know it?"

Frank nodded. "I thought it was abandoned."

"Lucky for you, it isn't. The woman is from the bitter water clan. She's called Yanaha, but her family name is Todachine."

"How long are they keeping Emilio?" Frank asked.

Yiska squinted again for an answer, this time

somewhere on Frank's face. "You're not asking for the case, are you," Yiska stated more than questioned.

Frank shook his head.

"I don't know."

"I am sorry."

"I know." Yiska looked back at the radishes, only nodding when Frank spoke the Navajo word for "goodbye."

"Hágoónee'."

CHAPTER
4

The hogan still seemed deserted to Frank, even as he approached the door, which was no more than a Navajo-style blanket, its original colors and pattern faded by wind and sun. The structure of the hogan smelled of earth the same as Yiska's, but instead of an obvious differentiation between the earth and a human-made structure, the bitter water clan woman's hogan appeared to rise from the ground naturally, like a mountain or tree. It was no more than a mound of dried, reddish mud, at least on the outside.

Frank greeted the owner in both Navajo and Papago as he only knew that she was tied to both tribes and nothing more about her.

She answered in neither.

As Frank called Yá'át'éé for the second time, a woman's face appeared to the side of the blanket like a spontaneous growth.

"Yes?" the dark round face asked.

Frank had expected a more conventional response. "Are you Yanaha Todachine?"

The woman didn't agree or disagree in any visible way but squinted at Frank, remaining mostly curtained. She nodded at last, making a small noise he couldn't interpret as anything other than an auditory extension of her nod.

"I'm Detective Frank Silva. I'm here because I need to know if you sold cow hoof powder to anyone recently."

Yanaha nodded. "A few months ago a note without any name or phone number or address was pinned to this blanket. The note asked for the powder to be delivered to a specific place. I'll bet you want to know where." Yanaha grinned, revealing a missing tooth on her upper row.

Frank nodded.

"I had my boy deliver it at night
to a cactus plant."

"Where was this cactus? Was it near the old Salt Bingo?"

Yanaha nodded. "The note described a strange cactus, shaped like a top hat near the place where they leave flowers."

"Did you keep the note?" Frank asked.

Yanaha shook her head. "I don't keep paper I don't need."

Frank watched the old woman's face for a few seconds, realizing she had nothing else to offer him as her expression hardened into a stillness that would only budge with another question, and he couldn't think of another one that would lead him anywhere.

"Thank you for your help." Frank watched the old woman disappear behind the blanket, surprising him again with a traditional Navajo "goodbye."

The cactus was shaped like something a man might have worn on his head for a very formal evening out in early- to mid-nineteenth century America or Europe. Other than this odd shape, nothing else stood out about the plant.

The unofficial name of the "top hat" cactus was Desert Lettuce as vegetation ruffled around its base. Although it was one of the odder desert plants Frank had seen, what stood out was who had historically used the plant for medicine. A "cave people" who assimilated into Papago society once lived in caves near the reservation and used the white "blood" of the Desert Lettuce as a healing liquid.

After so many years as a detective, Frank considered himself an informal student of human nature, and this education had taught him that people generally chose points of reference with personal meaning. The strange cactus was more than a random drop-off spot, especially when there were plenty of other reference points to offer. Frank guessed the person who ordered the cow hoof powder was either a descendant of the cave people or a knowledgeable fan of a dead culture.

Frank knew the place where the cave people once lived. There was a legend trickled down through his family that his great-great-great-great-great grandfather on his mother's side had lived in the same caves. Even so, he had never visited the place that was home to ancestors who never even had a formal tribal name. They were simply known as outsiders.

The series of caves ranged from thumbprint depressions to deeper cavities, Frank discovered as he wandered into several of the openings. He stopped at the sixth cave mouth, a generous pocket of darkness that would have been a perfect hiding spot, particularly if you were evading the law. Any of the deeper cavities would have sufficed for this purpose; however, the sixth opening proved his theory correct with the remains of an ancient altar—ancient only in its configuration, not in the materials used to build it.

Though he had never seen the tangible form of such an altar, his mother's mother had told him enough to close the gap between the rough image in his imagination and the altar made of painted rocks. The rocks were coated in vivid blues and greens and pinks and yellows as he had visualized. It was the first intact remnant of the Outsider tribe in the cave system he had seen. In three of the first five caves, there was scattered rubble of stone altars, and any paint had been worn away over time. This meant the altar in the sixth cave was recently erected.

If it really was the killer who built the altar, Frank had to remind himself how long it took to make his way to the cave. It was a mental hurdle. He hadn't simply walked in, even though in one sense he had. About half of the time when a case had unraveled too easily, it was too good to be true, so Frank was wary of things such as intact altars that should have been reduced to dust more than a century ago.

Other than the minimalist altar, which climbed to the point of a multifaceted triangle, each face representing sky, earth, and water, there was no evidence of human presence. He carefully removed a couple of the top rocks, reverencing them for a moment in his hands before bagging them as evidence.

Moving into heavier shades of darkness further in, he smelled something. The scent returned him to a more familiar world on the reservation, but even more precisely, there was something floral and feminine in the smell. He followed it to its strongest concentration, pursuing it until it broke down. Collecting nothing more than the perfumed air, Frank turned around. He had smelled the perfume before, but the memory was a fog he could only pass through. He couldn't contain it.

One thing was certain. Whoever carried the perfumed scent was most likely the altar's architect as there wasn't so much as a spray of graffiti or empty beer can in any of the caves to indicate regular visitors to this remote part of the desert. He looked at the rocks through the plastic, wondering if they had anything to confess.

Frank stood outside the crime lab where a tech interrogated the two painted stones with a precise, delicate torture. Down the hall, Arturo applied a similarly delicate torture to Russell. In his peripheral vision, Frank noticed a figure moving. He knew it was Arturo.

Frank abandoned his watch at the lab door, following Arturo into an interrogation room. Russell sat bent over a table, his usually sturdy, athletic frame hunched under the weight of the stress and exhaustion. As part of tailing the boy, Arturo had followed Russell a week before to the perfumed cave; however, that trip didn't make sense until Frank gave Arturo the context of his own findings. Across the table, Frank recognized someone grappling with himself. Dark circles rimmed Russell's eyes.

"I needed to find out for myself," Russell began, sighing through his nose.

Frank resisted his impatience, letting the boy speak at his own pace.

"Regina asked me to train her to hunt at night in the desert."

"Regina Acuna?" Frank glanced sideways at Arturo, who nodded and shrugged. Frank's mind raced around for a motive but only bumped into the wall of disbelief that someone he had known to be decent her whole life could be capable of such a violent crime. Surrounding this wall was only the fog of the same general hatred that everyone on the reservation held for the cartel.

"She wanted to kill her own food. I mean she's coach's lady, so I just thought she wanted to shoot like him." Russell shrugged limply. "She seemed to know the area around the casino pretty well, so she wanted to hunt out there."

Frank hung on the word "casino," his mind racing around for a motive.

"Can I get a soda or something?" Russell asked.

Arturo stood up. "Sure, I'll get it."

"So you needed to find out for yourself whether she did it," Frank added.

Russell nodded.

The door opened, but before Arturo could shut the door behind him, the lab tech appeared, motioning to Frank, who joined him in the hall.

"Regina Acuna," the tech said.

The two words were all Frank needed. He nodded, returning to a silent interrogation room where Russell sipped a cherry cola and Arturo leaned back in his chair, watching the boy's movements with folded arms.

"Russell, it was Regina's fingerprints on the painted stones in the cave," Frank said.

Arturo leaned forward. "Russell, I'm sorry."

The boy mouthed something at the table. Frank guessed an obscenity.

"Only mother I've ever had," Russell continued, speaking to the table.

"We're not trying to take that away, here." Arturo leaned across the table, his palms outward in a receptive gesture.

Russell wiped at his eyes with the back of his hand.

He could take down a man with a single arrow shot, but he was only a child. "The sooner we find her, the sooner we figure out how she got into this mess, Russell," Frank reassured.

The boy nodded, but it was reflexive, as mourning overcast his faraway expression.

"By the way, how did you know to look in the caves?" Frank followed a groove in the table's veneer back and forth with his thumbnail, a reflexive habit that also focused his thoughts.

"I was hunting at night and ran into Regina. Her face was messed up. I hadn't seen her in like a week because she moved out from coach's house and I was back home with my old man. I just asked if she was okay, and she said she was and said not to worry—that if things got really bad, she'd go live in the caves. She was kind of smiling, so I thought she was joking. I looked up the caves and found them. We didn't talk long."

"What do you mean 'messed up?'" Frank asked, wondering if Emilio's anger at the cartel had spilled into his marriage. "Did Emilio ever get physical with Regina?"

Frank checked Arturo's response. The other detective nodded, his eyes never leaving Russell. His expression didn't register the surprise Frank's did. The detective realized he had already heard Russell's answers to the questions, but he needed to hear the answers directly himself. He had often observed the same question asked by different detectives producing new or elaborated responses.

Russell straightened, and Frank noticed an energy returning to his eyes. "Hell no."

Frank believed the boy, but someone had beaten up Regina.

"Russell, we need to find Regina to find out who hurt her," Arturo pressed.

"It wasn't coach. He couldn't have done it," Russell continued his defense.

"We don't believe he could either, but like Detective Vega said, we need to find Regina. Is there anything else besides what's in the cave that might help find her?" Frank asked.

Frank could see Russell's eyes searching some space beyond the interrogation room as the boy looked down through the table, but he ultimately shook his head. "No, nothing."

Arturo staked out the cave while Frank visited the upstairs apartment in Burning Rock where he witnessed the priest enter. According to the landlord, Regina had moved out more than a week before, so it was back to the caves where Frank relieved Arturo. The Feds retrieved Arturo from the caves for the useless formality of killing on paper the already dead beheading cases. Arturo had no eleventh-hour reason to resurrect the cases.

While Arturo was occupied, Frank camped out near the caves, watching the quiet, still mouths of these portals to the past, and in the case of one, to the present. For three days he watched this stillness. Arturo joined him on the second day of the watch, but his presence stirred only conversation.

"We've been seen," Frank said on the third night.

"Or she's moved on, or never stayed here in the first place." Arturo spoke between chews of cholla cactus buds.

"Could be. If she doesn't show up tonight that's the end of it. Bureau of Indian Affairs is starting to scratch at our door anyway."

Arturo made a noise in the back of his throat that sounded like a half-groan, half-grunt.

"Only dance partner we've got and they always

lead. Even you know that by now." Frank ignored a second groan-grunt, buffering the hard, flat face of a rock against his head with a folded blanket. He closed his eyes, but even in the black void where it was always midnight, Regina's face broke up the darkness into shadow and light, like a candle lit inside of a cave.

CHAPTER
5

Father Harris sat alone in the front pew of the sanctuary of St. Ignatius—as still as the dead.

Frank sat down behind the priest, clearing his throat.

The priest turned around. "I knew I'd get you near the altar eventually, detective." Father Harris smiled, mostly with his tea-colored eyes.

"Don't get too excited, Padre. May I?" Frank nodded at the spot next to Father Harris, who moved over.

"The last time I sat this close, I was with my grandmother," Frank noted. "She always had to be in the first or second pew. To my great disappointment." Frank reciprocated the priest's smiling eyes.

"Welcome back." Father Harris deferred a

sober expression to the one above the altar whose eyes sorrowed permanently.

Frank pretended not to notice. His lapsed Catholicism extended back to adolescence when he chose to skip his Confirmation in favor of smoking his first joint with a cousin who ironically wound up becoming a mission priest down in Sinaloa. "I'm here about Regina."

Father Harris's eyes remained on the sorrowful figure on the crucifix. "I figured you weren't through with me, but I don't know much." Father Harris smiled only with his eyes this time.

"You don't know much, or you can't tell me much?" Frank searched the rest of the priest's face for more than what was on his lips, but his expression was a tight seal over Regina's secrets and the secrets of thousands of other souls, no doubt.

"I don't know where Regina is right now, and that's all I can tell you."

Frank was more than mildly irritated at the priest's situational omniscience. He would have defended Regina's innocence was he not sitting on something incriminating.

"I saw you visiting her in Burning Rock." Frank hoped this dynamite would blow up the wall protecting whatever the priest knew. Father Harris's face remained still, placid even.

"So you followed me, detective." The priest continued speaking to Frank through the god-man hanging over the altar.

"After you suddenly joined the border militia, I was curious. And you're one of the best shots around here."

"Like Emilio and Russell and Graham," Father Harris added.

Frank nodded.

"Do you have any evidence Regina killed those men?" Father Harris asked.

Frank circled the murder scene in his mind, spreading out from there to the Carlos Rios memorial, then to the cave with the altar.

"In my mind, there's a fine point on her guilt, since the only name I came away with—the only fingerprints I came away with—were hers."

"And her motive?" Father Harris asked.

Frank sighed, shaking his head. "Only the same one we all have on the Rez. It's a poison that's reached our blood and is going to cause a war. Might be tomorrow. Might be in ten years, but it's a toxin that's been building up for too long, and it'll kill the body eventually—and our body includes the cartel passing through our lands."

Frank glanced at Father Harris, whose gaze fixed on the crucifix over the altar. Frank noticed fatigue passing across the priest's face like brief cloud cover on an otherwise sunny day.

"What were you doing at Regina's apartment, Father?" Frank continued his momentum, hoping to catch the priest unguarded while he was still caught up in Frank's last comment.

"Hearing her general confession," Father Harris replied matter-of-factly, his eyes meeting Frank's, serious, but no longer cast with a tired heaviness.

Frank knew this meant Regina had spilled the entire contents of her soul, past and present.

"Detective, I'm not trying to tell you your job, but I'm also a student of human behavior, and it seems to me you're focusing a lot on cold details that should lead from point A to the killer, as opposed to your primary suspect, who up until now was an innocent person in your community. You've known Regina her whole life. Why not start there?"

The last sentence struck Frank particularly because it contained a balance of the procedural with the personal. It was the latter, however, that he had not reconciled to the former. He realized he had not allowed himself to illuminate.

"You pin the general motive of an angry citizen of the reservation on an individual before you consider there might be a much narrower cause." Father Harris folded his hands, but it was more a loose tangle of fingers than a carefully arranged formation in prayer.

The priest's light eyes glowed against his skin with a radiant energy that Frank couldn't help but notice. Father Harris's advice was as much passionate monologue as it was a logical persuasion, inspiring even more certitude in Frank of Regina's guilt.

"Seems almost like you want me to find her," Frank said.

"Maybe I do." The priest turned his body toward the detective. "Maybe she needs to be found."

Priests didn't speak in "maybes," or perhaps they did, and he hadn't observed enough men who wore the collar to know any different. He was used to a natural confidence in black-and-white thinking from the priests he knew, including Father Harris, but in this priest's eyes, Frank saw a struggle. He had seen the same mixture of exhaustion and fight in Russell's face. It was the poison of war spreading its sickness. Even if Regina was guilty, no matter her motive, Frank realized that her victims would make her a martyr to the people. A martyr much bigger than the one that stood at the border with its cold, hollow eyes; one of flesh and blood that would inspire even more violence.

Frank left the priest to his solitude. Father Harris was right. Frank hadn't even registered his own shock at knowing someone he still thought of as a child had killed with a premeditated hand. He prided himself on this kind of detachment in his casework, but that's not what was needed now.

Regina's mother was born in a brothel and died in one nearly five years before Frank pursued Regina for murder. Regina's father, a drunk like Russell's dad, died from his life inside the bottle when his daughter was nineteen, leaving her with only memories of a childhood where she was on her own. He hadn't abused her, but she was neglected. It was a well-distributed fact among those that knew her. This included Frank. Regina's only sibling, an older brother, was imprisoned in California for selling stolen car parts. He was the only one in Regina's family who had left the reservation, and he wasn't even a free man. Varying strains of alcoholism; from a drunk, maternal uncle stumbling off a bridge, to a paternal aunt beaten to death by an alcoholic boyfriend, had claimed Regina's extended family. That left no one to question in that bloodline. She was cursed, but only in the way that everyone on the reservation was cursed.

It was only in considering these morbid details of Regina's family tree that Frank understood how impersonal solving cases had become for him. Impersonal worked well enough when he was solving the same simple Rez cases over and over, but this bred laziness, such as generalizing motives like the one he attached to Regina. As the priest said, he had to start with Regina, not end with her.

Regina was born and raised on the Rez, but she had bucked the trend set by her family with good grades in school and even a business degree from Arizona State. She was the first and only person to attend college in her family.

Somewhere though, she abruptly turned a

corner. It was more than a family curse or the same simmering anger of the Rez masses that launched the careful planning of two murders, which meant knowing when the traffickers would pass by the casino and how much poison it would take to kill two adult men with a single arrow shot in each man.

Frank considered what he knew. A woman left her husband and moved to a small town nearby, but after the murders, instead of moving even further away, she continued showing up around the Rez. She didn't land in any one place permanently but stayed on the move, hunting at night in the desert, building an altar in an ancestor cave. He didn't understand the altar yet, but it didn't matter. She still felt like the Rez was her home, and though she remained on the fringes like a scared, wounded animal, she wouldn't leave but wouldn't turn herself in either. A boy saw that her face was mangled, and he could see this even in the darkness, so the beating must have been bad. An epiphany lit on this theory.

Now, all Frank had to do was catch the wounded animal before it got a notion to do something stupid like bolt for good.

•))) · ✦ · (((•

Regina stood under the light next to the old Salt Bingo when Frank and Arturo spotted her on the third night of their second stakeout. Frank knew she had to show up eventually because Russell had seen her hunting in the area recently, and since she had decided to stay local, she was forced to live off-grid, under the radar, finding her meals at the end of an arrow.

She looked like an actor on stage under the spotlight, about to deliver a climactic monologue. Scars marked each feature of her face, from chin to forehead. It was as if these pieces of flesh were all stitched into place in this way. She was a petite woman, but she seemed like a child standing alone, helpless in the spot where she killed two men. She stared somewhere on the ground, but her gaze fell with precision. She didn't flinch when Frank and Arturo approached.

"I was watching you even while you watched me. Russell taught me that. We can adjust our senses to the darkness when we have to. We're animals too." Regina pulled her eyes away at last from the ground. Her lips trembled. It was the only part of her that did.

"Regina, I know how you got those." Frank pointed to his own cheek.

The trembling increased. Her upper teeth restrained her lower lip. Her left hand formed a fist at her side as if in protest of her exposed vulnerability.

"I know it was Jorge Mercado that did that to you. He's a narc, but you obviously knew that." Frank paused, but Regina stilled up to her eyes. "It happened on the footpath. Maybe you were night hunting or visiting Rios, the symbolic patron of your casino. It made sense you used the stolen arrows and poisoned them. You'd become a good shot with an arrow by then, and being able to use the arrows that Rios used was the cherry on top. It was a way to stick it to the Mexicans even harder since they've always tried to take our land, even in Rios's time. It was a way to represent the roots of our people, even in a violent act. The poison was a way to do this too. Our people haven't used that poison in a hundred years. It was a way to kill them fast if you weren't going to use bullets," Frank said, his eyes tunneling behind his words into Regina.

Regina shuddered a nod, releasing her lower lip along with a hard puff of breath and noise like a soft grunt. "I loved that place. The museum." Regina unclenched her fist as she spoke. "I used to wander through there after work. It gave me peace when things were going bad with Emilio."

"So you knew the layout pretty well," Arturo added.

Regina nodded, her eyes wet and lips trembling unchecked. She opened her mouth to say something but grabbed her lower lip again, releasing it almost in the same instant. "I never meant to steal. But then I-I never meant to . . ." Regina looked down at the ground, then at her stomach, folding her arms over it protectively.

Frank thought he saw the same understanding of something unspoken in Arturo's eyes.

"You're pregnant," Frank stated more than asked, hoping Arturo would stay quiet about any question of paternity.

Regina continued looking at her stomach, her body visibly shaking.

Frank understood now how much was at stake.

Regina nodded, her head down. Her hands were now both clenched over her belly. "This is the only home I know. I couldn't leave, but I didn't know how to stay after what I did."

"So you've been a ghost," Frank said, wanting to comfort a murder suspect for the first time in thirty-four years. "But you left us clues. The arrow in the floor. The altar."

Regina still clutched at her stomach with fisted hands, though the fists had loosened. "They weren't supposed to be clues. I hid the arrow in the floor because I wasn't sure where else to hide them. I was the only one with access to the casino, and the altar was a gift I left for my ancestors when I moved out of that cave. I never thought anyone would find either."

Frank wondered if that was true, or if somehow Regina hoped to be drawn out. She hadn't made it easy, but maybe that was the point. Maybe if someone found these clues, it meant she was supposed to give herself up.

"How did you know how much poison to use and when the traffickers would pass through here?" Arturo asked.

Frank was just as curious about the answers to Arturo's questions, only he was more patient than the younger detective and wanted those questions to form more naturally. He wanted to follow Regina's lead.

Regina flattened her hands against her stomach. "I hunted the biggest game I could find, taking them down with the poison over and over until I felt confident I could do it. And I waited for those men to pass by." Regina's words wobbled out of trembling lips. She closed her eyes. "I knew eventually they would pass by. I had seen them many times. Men like Jorge. I knew they had an arrangement with the previous owner. They paid him off to use the Salt Bingo as a point of reference through all of this nothing." Regina pointed at the darkness beyond the spray of light. "I went up to that rooftop every night for five nights, and on the fifth night -" Regina stopped herself, her eyes on her stomach. "On that night -" Regina collapsed to her knees, her arms limp at her sides.

Frank waited, nudging Arturo, who started to say something to the young woman. Frank knew that after so many years of similar moments that what he waited for would come.

Regina finally looked up, shaking, though her eyes held firm on Frank. "On the fifth night I killed them. Those men." Regina spoke the last two words with closed eyes, dropping all the way to the ground, her body curled toward her growing belly.

Frank and Arturo pulled her back up, but she leaned against Frank and closed her eyes, letting the tears drain and the detectives lead her away from the only real light for a mile in every direction.

·»)· ✦ ·(((·

Frank and Arturo watched the border from a distance, but not so far they couldn't see Emilio, Russell, Graham, Father Harris—among other militia members—and even Yiska preparing for the ceremony.

"At least we're in plainclothes," Arturo remarked.

"We're unofficial security for an unofficial ceremony, so why should our clothes be any more official?" Frank said.

"Don't see why we're here even unofficially. The cartel won't ever show up at the border in daylight. They'll find out about this, and those bastards will roll more heads in the dead of night." Arturo frowned. "And Regina will have her baby in prison."

"Well, then I'm glad we're here, whatever the reason." Frank adjusted his bolo tie and raised the silver skull of a bull toward his throat.

"You thinking about joining the militia?" Arturo asked.

"I am." Frank's tone was reflexive, but he felt the full weight of both words. He was absorbed by Emilio at the top of a ladder, nearly as tall as the unearthly metal figure with the hollow eyes. A few hundred men and women clustered tightly around the ladder, their eyes watching Emilio's every move. Emilio placed a crown of gold flowers on top of The Martyr's head.

Silver letters twisted from some sort of metal followed the curve of the crown above the flowers.

Frank narrowed his eyes to read. The letters spelled "REGINA."

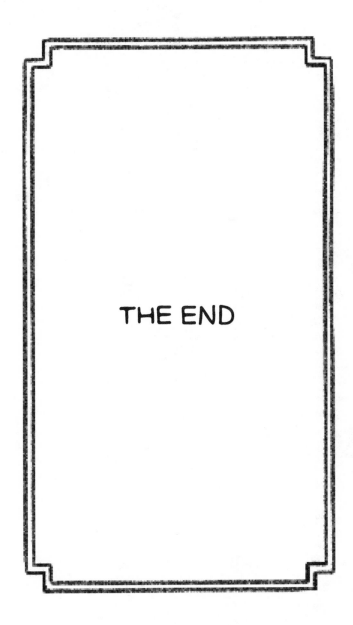

THE END